D1558471

Meet The All Stars

Nick

Amira

Carla

Flo

Juan

Carlos

Kareem

Lucy

Lacy

Larry

Dedication

I dedicate this book to my illustrator and partner in this journey, Dale Tangeman. He gave the Hometown All Stars life and believes as much as I do that we possess the ability to reach and help countless kids across the country, if not the world!
The journey all authors follow is a road filled with potholes and speed bumps, but along the way, we meet many people who help and support us. That journey can and should be as fulfilling as getting your actual work to its intended audience. The Hometown All Stars are blessed and continue to find ongoing help every day.
I am so grateful to everyone who collaborated to make Amira Can Catch great: Susan Barnett, Lisa Pingelski, Cecily Paterson, Cevin Bryerman, Marshall Karp, David Kaplan, Anita Lock, Tracy Chapman, Starsky Robinson, Kevin Barnett at Aural Studios for assisting with our audiobook recordings, Arturo Aguilar, MK, Jenna Jacoby, Megan Frandino, and Sondra Buono. Forever, and as always: Brittany and Jeff Bearden, Brian Mast, and my left and right hands, Sandi Armstrong and Darlene Foucher. Finally, to my main assistant, my son, Joey Christofora—age 11.

1. Baseball 2. T-Ball 3. Kid's 4. Children's 5. Educational 6. Fun 7. Multi-Culture 8. Catching 9. New Kid in School 10. Syria 11. Refuge 12. Teammate 13. Refugee Camp

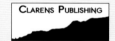

CLARENS PUBLISHING

ISBN 978-0-9863493-3-1

Library of Congress Control Number:

2017935639

Moms traditionally say that you can't play catch in the house, but if you roll up two socks, or maybe get three socks, all of your family can sit on the couch and chair and play catch with your socks after dinner.

Printed in the United States of America

The Hometown All Stars
Amira Can Catch

Dale and I are very grateful for your purchase of this book. We want to say thank you! Our goal from the inception has been to help get books into more kids' hands. We wanted them to be educational, both in English and in sports know-how. We wanted them to be fun and inspirational—read-more-than-once kind of books. We hope you enjoy them. If you are so inclined, please feel free to post a review on social media.

Sincerely,

Kevin Christofora-Author Dale Tangeman-Illustrator

When I got to school today, there was a new girl in our class. She was standing with our teacher, Mrs. Mayer. "Class, we have a new student," she said. "Her name is Amira, and she is from Syria. She has come a long way to get here. Make sure you all introduce yourself and make her feel welcome."

1.

Amira sat at the empty desk next to me. She looked a little nervous being in a new school. I think I would be a little nervous, too. Amira had trouble spelling her words and adding her numbers. I asked her if she needed help.

"Yes, I would like help very much, thank you. When I lived in the refugee camp, I didn't have school," she said. I told her it would be okay and that I would help. Then, I changed the subject and asked her if she would to like to play baseball at lunchtime with me. She had a big smile. "Yes, please."

Amira told us how lucky we were to have this much food every day. At her last camp, three kids had to share the same amount of food that we got for lunch.

"Oh, pickles! Yum! In Syria, we made the best pickles ever," she said. Most of us never ate our pickles, because they were green and they looked like rubber. Since Amira liked pickles, we all tried one, and we soon found out that we liked them, too!

3

After lunch, I asked Amira what a camp is.

"I call it a camp, like when you sleep in the woods with a tent. The real name is a refugee camp. It is where all the families live who have lost their houses and have nowhere else to go. We all set up our tents for sleeping and called it our campground."

Today went so fast. It was already the end of the day. I ran and gave Amira a map to baseball practice.

Yay, she made it! I was so happy that Amira came to practice. I introduced her to the whole team. I told her it was okay if she didn't remember all our names. "You can just call us by our numbers. We all know our numbers! You can say, 'Good hit, 12,' or 'Good catch, 8!' We'll know who you mean."

"Let's get this practice going!" Coach greeted us with a big smile. "Welcome, Amira! The team has told me all about you. I am so happy you came today."

"They told me all about you, too, sir," Amira replied.

"Please, just call me Coach!" He presented Amira with her jersey. "Today, you can be number 24. That's Willie Mays's number."

Coach got us all together and asked if we liked throwing and pitching from the last practice. "Yes!" we all shouted. We started walking around like windmills. Amira was joining in and laughing.

"Amira, I see you are going to fit in just fine with these silly characters." Coach chuckled. "Now, come check out this baseball card! Willie Mays was famous for more than being a great hitter. He was amazing at catching pop-fly balls, too. In the 1956 World Series, he ran back toward the homerun wall and caught a ball on the run, over his shoulder, and saved the game. His nickname was 'Say Hey Willie Mays'. It even rhymes. Now, let's go learn how to catch a ball, and maybe one day, you can be just like Willie Mays."

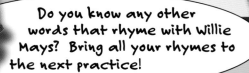

Do you know any other words that rhyme with Willie Mays? Bring all your rhymes to the next practice!

Carlos had the white hat from last practice. He was the leader today! He led us out to the pitcher's mound to start our warm-ups. "Who wants a hot dog?" he asked. We all raised our hands.

He laughed and said, "Down 1-2-3." He tricked us into doing stretches! We did all our warm-ups, and then, it was time for our run.

Carlos gave up the white hat to Juan. "Follow me!" Juan said.
"We are going to sing 'Peanut Butter Jelly Time' at every base," he said. It sounded like fun to me.
"Peanut Butter Jelly at first, Peanut Butter Jelly at second, Peanut Butter Jelly at third, and Peanut Butter Jelly on home plate."

After running, Coach split us up into groups. I was with Amira and Kareem. "Welcome to the catching station," Coach said. "Notice that each of you has two little circles. This is for a reason. To catch the ball, you do not stand straight. You stand diagonal!" He showed us how to bend our knees and to hold our hands with our palms up. "This is your READY position," he said. "We will be READY on every pitch and every swing of the bat."

"We are going to learn three types of catches! The first is for a GROUND BALL. In your READY position, place your glove with the fingertips DOWN to the ground," Coach instructed.
He showed us how the ball can roll right up into your glove like a ramp. It was so easy!

Don't try to trap the ball. Don't make a train tunnel...or the ball will go through the tunnel.

READY POSITION

THROWING POSITION

"Okay, let's do it! Get in your READY positions," Coach said. "Lacy! Here we go. Let's show Amira and Nick how to do this!"

After Lacy got in position, Coach said, "That is a nice READY position. I know you were at the last practice where we learned to throw. Don't forget to look like the letter T and make a nice throw back to me after you catch the ball."

"Nick, are you ready? It's your turn!"
"Here we go...Nice catch! Now, throw it back to me. Remember: turn sideways, look like the letter T, point your glove at me, rock back, rock forward, and throw." I followed all of his instructions, and my ball went right into his glove. Coach said, "Awesome, good job, Nick!"

"Next!" Coach called. "Amira, it's your turn!
Get in your READY position...and here it comes...Nice catch! Now,
throw it back to me." POW! "I think you have done this before!"

"Now we're cooking...Let's do it again. Lacy, are you ready? Palms up, FINGERS DOWN. No trapping, no choo-choo train tunnels!"

Coach asked the three of us, "Say it with me. All of you, together! FINGERS DOWN, palms up, no choo-choo train tunnels! No choo-choo train tunnels!" He asked us why we thought choo-choo train tunnels were bad. I responded, "Because trains go through tunnels and we want to catch the ball."

18

"Good job, All Stars. That's how you do it. Now, let's go to the next station, and I don't mean the train station."

Coach named this second station, the Say Hey Willie Mays' POP-FLY-Station. As he was talking, Coach caught all of us fooling around. He said, "Pay attention, All Stars, or you're going to have to run around the whole baseball field."

Coach continued...He showed us that for **POP FLY** balls, you put your glove straight up over your head. It should be lined up so your glove is over your nose when you look up. Your other hand goes behind the glove to help hold the ball in it. This is called catching with **TWO HANDS**. Move your feet to get under the ball, and keep your laser-beam eyes on the red stitches. Watch the ball go into your glove.

At first, Coach was throwing the ball right to our gloves. After that, he made them go higher and even higher still. This was big-time fun.

Coach was really not bad at all. He was actually, as they say, "weaving a basket" on purpose to sneak in more exercise for the kids without them knowing it.

I don't think Coach was too good at this drill. He could not get the ball to us. We had to keep chasing the ball, moving left, then right, then back, then in closer. He had us running all over the field, trying to catch it. This drill went fast, and the pop flies just kept coming one after another. We got a lot of chances to make a lot of catches.

"Are you tired yet?" Coach asked. "Let's walk over to the dugout and grab some water."
He told us that this was the third and last practice drill today and that it would be the best one of all!
"This is how we PLAY CATCH. The best part is that when you play catch, you get to play with a friend! Drop your water bottles, everyone pick a teammate, and line up on the first base line with a ball and your glove. We already learned FINGERS DOWN and POP FLIES. Now, we are going to learn FINGERS UP! This is for all the balls in the middle."

"Here is the secret," Coach said. "If the ball is above your waist, your glove should be FINGERS UP. When the ball is below your waist, your glove should be FINGERS DOWN."
We started throwing the ball to each other. "Catch the ball, turn sideways, and throw the ball back to your teammate." He reminded us never to throw the ball when your teammate is not looking at you.

We all gathered at the pitcher's mound.
"What was your favorite part today?" Coach asked. We all started shouting out different answers: No Trains, Choo-choo! Catching and Throwing! Chugga Chugga! Ice Cream!

"All Stars, you did a great job at catching today! I am very proud of you.
I can't wait for the next practice. It's called Pizza Pie Day!
I know you're going to love it! Now, let's go to the bleachers!"

"Amira, how did you get so good?" I asked her.
"We had lots of time to throw and catch when we were living at the campgrounds. We didn't have many other toys to play with."

"Alright, All Stars, are you ready for some questions?"
1. What is the name of the game?
2. Why do we play it?
3. What is Willie Mays' number?
4. Who likes train tunnels?

"C'mon, man! Tunnels? Who said they liked train tunnels? Who raised their hand? Everyone who raised their hand...you have to give me a card back." Coach laughed "C'mon, all you silly choo-choo tunnel lovers, hand 'em over! Give me a card back, you silly kids!"

29

Coach's Special Questions

5. **What was Amira's favorite class in school?**
6. **How many pop flies did Amira catch?**
7. **When you are in your READY POSITION, what do you do?**
8. **Who can tell me what the red wristband says?**

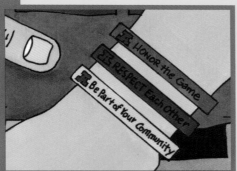

9. **Can anyone tell me where Amira is from?**

I hope you all have taken the time to talk to our new friend and teammate and find out all about her. You get a 'Respect' wristband for getting to know her better.

10. Who wants ice cream?

Wow! If Amira had to share her lunch at her old home, I wonder if she ever had ice cream, especially after playing baseball.

My mom was talking to someone new after practice.
"Nick, this is Amira's mom and dad, Mr. and Mrs. Tuncel. Amira is going to be on the team all the time now."
I was so happy. Amira and I high-fived each other. I said, "See you in school tomorrow, teammate!"

What Does it Mean to be American?

Christopher Columbus discovered North America in 1492. Years later, many other European countries began to move from their home countries to this newly discovered land—the United States—in hopes of new opportunities and a different life.

After the American Revolution, the United States won its independence, and the citizens of the United States became known as Americans. They now took care of and protected their new land and homes. Soon, they started new families, and babies were growing up to help on the farms and factories.

The new generation had no memory of the countries their parents and grandparents had come from. They were born in America; they were instantly Americans, citizens of the United States of America by birth. However, their parents taught them never to forget where they came from and to always be proud of the country their relatives came from. That is called your nationality.

You can be an American, and live in America, and still have the same blood in your body from your parents and grandparents who were born in another part of the world. You can be Chinese-American, you can be an Italian-American, you can be an Irish-American, or you can even be a Native American if all your family came from America.

Coach Kevin is an American whose ancestors come from many different nationalities. His grandparent's parents were from all over Europe—Ireland, England, the Netherlands, and Italy. Where is your family from? It has been over 500 years since Christopher Columbus discovered America. Families from all over the world are still trying to move to America.

America is considered one of the greatest countries in the world. It is known as the "land of opportunity." Opportunity means that America offers the freedom to work for pay to make as much money as you can to get ahead and to help build a better life. All kids have the right to go to school and get a good education. And, every American over the age of 18 gets to vote for the president. Some other countries do not allow voting.

Today, America is made up of people from all around the world. When you put them all together, it is called a "Melting Pot." America is a melting pot! Put them in the pot, and mix them up. What do you get? You get an American who is proud to be an American citizen, and you also have an American who is proud of their nationality. Americans love the land they live on, and they have the right to protect it. What it means to be an American is in the hearts of the people who, in their struggles and heartaches, in their joys and triumphs, fight for America and fight to be American every day.

A citizen is a person from a place they were born, raised, or live. The Hometown All Stars are citizens of Woodstock, NY, USA. Where are you a citizen of?

Here are some new words we have learned in this book.

Recess, Refugee Camp, Rhyme, Pickles, Squat, Ramp, Tunnel, Play Catch, Pop Fly, Ground Ball, Ready Position, Throwing Position

German • Italian
Braille • Spanish • Chinese • Japanese • Korean
Arabic • English

All Hometown All Stars books are available in 13 languages!

G• Russian • Curacao • Georgian • Poland •

There are a total of 10 Golden Gloves in this book.